Cyberpals
According to
Kaley

by
Dian Curtis Regan

DARBY
CREEK
PUBLISHING

For Sally Hefley,
my dear friend and international cyberpal

Text copyright © 2006 by Dian Curtis Regan
Design by Kelly Rabideau

Cataloging-in-Publication

Regan, Dian Curtis.
Cyberpals according to Kaley / by Dian Curtis Regan.
        p. ; cm.
ISBN-13: 978-1-58196-051-8
ISBN-10: 1-58196-051-4
Summary: Kaley Bluster is back! This time she's struggling with a Language Arts assignment to correspond via email with overseas "cyberpals," and she's looking for a nickname. As usual, the assignments provide entertainment for Mr. Serrano as he grades them.
1. Electronic mail messages—Juvenile fiction. 2. Nicknames—Juvenile fiction. 3. School children—Juvenile fiction. [1. Email—Fiction. 2. Nicknames—Fiction. 3. Elementary school students—Fiction.] I. Title. II. Author.
PZ7.R25854 Cy 2006
[Fic] dc22
OCLC: 65178317

DARBY CREEK PUBLISHING

Published by Darby Creek Publishing
7858 Industrial Parkway
Plain City, OH 43064
www.darbycreekpublishing.com

Printed in the United States of America

1 2 3 4 5 6 7 8 9 10

Grade 4
Language Arts

<u>Assignment</u>: Along with our unit on Letter Writing, I am adding a sub-unit on e-mail to give the class practice responding to "friendly letters."

We will participate with international schools around the world that use English in the classroom. Guidelines:

1. Choose a country that interests you from the list.
2. Pick a "cyberpal" from the participating school.
3. Write an introductory letter about yourself.
4. Be sure to greet your cyberpal in his or her native language.
5. Topics to write about: family, school, holidays, pets.

Please print out a hard copy of each e-mail for your assignment notebook so I can follow your e-mails and grade the project. Remember to use good e-mail etiquette.

Have fun!
Mr. Serrano

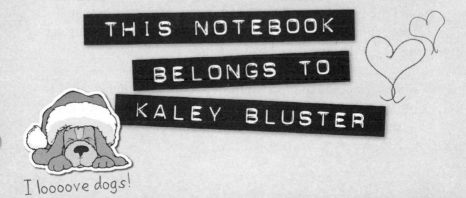

THIS NOTEBOOK
BELONGS TO
KALEY BLUSTER

I loooove dogs!

Kaley Bluster

Date: Monday, November 27
To: by.the.sea@escuela.net.ve
From: Kaley@flutter.edu
Subject: Greetings from your cyberpal!

Dear Adrian,

Buenos días from the USA!

Everyone in my class had to pick a country that sounded interesting. I picked Venezuela because all the other fourth graders started at the top of the list and chose countries beginning with A:

Africa, Algeria, Albania, Austria.

I started at the bottom and worked my way up. Venezuela was the first country I thought I could remember how to spell. (Forget "Zimbabwe." I had to look up the spelling six times just to type it as a bad example.)

(I was supposed to greet you in your native language, but I did not know how to say "USA" in Spanish.) (I didn't know how to say "good morning" either, but my teacher wrote it on the board for me.) (And for Shanay Wink, who is writing to someone in Argentina.)

After we turned in our "country of choice," my teacher, Mr. Serrano, connected us with our cyberpals.

I am not sure how Mr. S. found you. He said something about a stable of international schools seeking cyberpals in the United States.

I am sorry to hear that you go to school in a stable. Don't they have regular buildings there? Do you have to share the space with horses? That would be cool. A cow in the classroom would not.

Let me tell you about myself. I am nine years old and in the fourth grade at Mildred Flutter Elementary. (If you want to know who Mildred Flutter is, just ask!) (Ooops, I should say "who she WAS" since she is no more.) What I mean is that she died. (But it happened a long time ago, so I'm not trying to make you feel sorry for us at the school she left behind.) (There's a picture of her by the nurse's office, and she looked very old even when she wasn't dead.)

I have a baby brother named Matthew. He is pretty useless right now. Can't play games or watch videos with me. Ho hum.

My mother is a yoga instructor. Do you have yoga in your country?

My father works, too, but I don't know what he does. He leaves the house before I go to school and comes home just as Mom is dishing up dinner. ("Good timing," she always says, but then makes him clean up the kitchen.)

Oh, and my dad hates to wear ties, so he carries them in the car and puts one on before going into his office. He takes it off the minute he leaves and tosses it onto the backseat. (There's quite a pile now since I give him ties for every birthday and Christmas. It's the only "dad gift" I can ever think of.)

My father's building is downtown and is made of glass. I can see clouds in the windows when I stand on the sidewalk and look up. Sometimes I find coins that people have dropped while feeding the meter. Once, Cal (my annoying cousin) found a quarter. Me? Only pennies. So far. (What do you call coins in your country?)

My dad likes Fridays best because it's "casual day," and he doesn't have to wear a tie. Now you know more about my father than about me!

Well, our teacher told us to keep our introductory letters short. He probably should have been more specific.

Please write back and tell me about you.

Sincerely,
Kaley Bluster

Kaley,

Good start, albeit parentheses overkill. Not necessary to use them twelve times in one e-mail. Also, Africa is a <u>continent</u>, not a <u>country</u>.

Mr. Serrano

Mr. S,

Is "albeit" a real word or did you make it up?

Kaley

Kaley Bluster

Date: Tuesday, November 28
To: by.the.sea@escuela.net.ve
From: Kaley@flutter.edu
Subject: Anyone there?

Dear Adrian,

Did you get my e-mail? Are you going to write back?

I am the only one in class whose cyberpal did not answer. Shanay got a four-page e-mail from hers. She is flashing it around like she won an award. When I said I did not receive an answer, she gave me her pouty-sad look. Please write back. I do not like Shanay's pouty-sad look.

Shanay's pouty look

Here are questions in case you need something to write about:
1. How long did it take you to learn English?
2. Do you have to wear skirts to school? (The picture of Venezuela on page 58 in my social studies book shows girls in colorful skirts.)
3. Is it really summer all year round? (What I read on page 59.)

4. (Sorry about those parentheses. I can never get the blinking thingie in the right place to delete them. If I had a computer at home, like Cal, I'd know more about blinking thingies.) (Santa has been notified.)

PLEASE E ME BACK!!!!!!!!!
(Shanay is circling again.) ←oops, sorry.

Sincerely,
Kaley

My don't-get-me-this-for-Christmas list:

1. Socks
2. Underwear
3. Scented soap
4. Books about bugs (Cal. Last year.)
5. Pjs with TRUCKS on them
     (Cal. Again.) (Triple ewww.)

Kaley Bluster

Date: Tuesday, November 28
To: Kaley@flutter.edu
From: by.the.sea@escuela.net.ve
Subject: I heard ya the 1st time

Hey,
Watz ^?
Adrian here.
No one calls me that. :-<
My nickname is Lobo.
I was born in Detroit,
so my English is as good as yours.
I do NOT wear skirts to school.
I am a BOY. :-ll
Yes, aamof it is summer all year round.
No cold winters like Michigan.
In Spanish, we call the USA "Los Estados Unidos."
Coins are "las monedas."
Don't really care who Mildred Flutter is or was.
Same with yoga. dkdc
I got assigned to write to you.
Not crazy about it.
Especially since you called me a girl. :-r
bfn
Lobo ^..^

boys = YUCK

Mr. Serrano!!!!!!!!

You made a huge mistake!!!!!
I've been e-matched with
a boy instead of a girl!!!!!!!
Please quick find me somebody
else to write to!!!!!!

Kaley!!!!!

Kaley (!!!!),

Besides forgetting the unit on punctuation, in which we learned that exclamation points should be used as sparingly as parentheses, you obviously weren't listening when I told the class that some of you would have cyberpals of the opposite sex.

You'll do fine. Keep e-writing.
Mr. Serrano

P.S. "Albeit" is a real word. Look it up.

Mr. S,

I heard you say our cyberpal might be the opposite sex, albeit I did not know that meant it would be a BOY.

Sincerely,
Not a Happy E-writer

Kaley Bluster

Date: Wednesday, November 29
To: by.the.sea@escuela.net.ve
From: Kaley@flutter.edu
Subject: Ooooops . . . .

Dear Lobo,

I am sorry for thinking you're a girl. My
mother has a great-aunt named Adrian, and she
is a girl. (Actually, she is a lady—an old lady—
not a girl at all. But you get my point.)

↑
Great-aunt
Adrian

My teacher is making me write back to you,
even though you are a boy.

You write funny.
In short sentences.
Like this.
It looks like a poem.
But it does not rhyme.

Cal told me what your smile thingies meant.
(:-r) (Even though they weren't smiling). He
showed me how to stick little heads into my
letters, like this: ☺

And smile thingies like this: : *

Oh, wait, I think that means "kiss"!!!!!
NEVER MIND. ☹ ☹ ☹

I don't know what the letters by themselves mean: aamof,
dkdc, bfn. I figured out the first one: watz^ = what's up?
Since this is a school assignment, we have to use proper
English—which is good, since I'm probably the only one
who doesn't know e-lingo. (See previous message about not
having a computer at home.)

We're supposed to tell our cyberpals about American
holidays and about school in the USA, but since you were
born here, you already know these things, so I guess there's
no reason to keep cyberpal-ing.

We are also supposed to tell our cyberpals
about pets, but since I am the only fourth grader
in the entire universe who doesn't have a pet
(thanks to baby Matthew), I have nothing to
say on that topic.

One question: Why are you going to school in Venezuela if
you were born in Detroit?

I really like your nickname. It's triple cool! I think I'll get me
a nickname, too.

Sincerely,
Kal (nickname) ←Kal is cool^3!!!

P.S. Wait!!! "Kal" is too much like "Cal." (Who is a boy, in case you were wondering.) I'll have to come up with something else.

Mr. S,

May I please see the cyberpal list again?

Thank you,
Ley

Kaley,

Did the attached note come from you? It's signed "Ley," and I wasn't sure who that was.

It's okay to write to a different cyberpal, but first make sure you and Adrian mutually agree to stop e-writing.

Mr. Serrano

Kaley Bluster

Date: Wednesday, November 29
To: by.the.sea@escuela.net.ve
From: Kaley@flutter.edu
Subject: ???????

Dear Lobo,

Me. Again.

Is it okay with you if we stop e-writing? My teacher says you
have to "mutually agree"—whatever that means.

I have one more question before we say "adios." Where did
you get your nickname? What does it mean?

Yours truly,
Just Plain Kaley

Adios muchacho!

↑
just learned this
word from Ms. Bart,
our librarian

Kaley Bluster

Date: Wednesday, November 29
To: Kaley@flutter.edu
From: by.the.sea@escuela.net.ve
Subject: hasta la vista

Hey,
Okay by me to stop e-writing.
"Lobo" means "wolf" in Spanish.
My last name is Wolf. (^..^)
My mom is from Caracas, and my father is from Detroit.
They wanted me to know my mother's family.
That is why I am living in Venezuela.
Oh, and we don't say "adios" here, we say "ciao."
Since you're a cluebie when it comes to e-mail:
aamof = as a matter of fact
dkdc = don't know, don't care
bfn = bye for now
cluebie = clueless newbie
And since you'll probably ask . . .
"hasta la vista" means "see ya later."
Ciao,
Lobo ^..^

Lobo = lame-o

Kaley Bluster

Date: Wednesday, November 29
To: by.the.sea@escuela.net.ve
From: Kaley@flutter.edu
Subject: I have a great idea!!!!!

Dear Lobo,

First, my tongue is tired from trying to figure
out how to pronounce "ciao." Help!

Second, my last name is "Bluster." What is
the Spanish word for that? It might make
the perfect nickname for me.

ME
(with my tongue tied)

Hopefully,
Still Kaley

Kaley Bluster

Date: Wednesday, November 29
To: Kaley@flutter.edu
From: by.the.sea@escuela.net.ve
Subject: "Ciao" sounds like "chow"

Hey,
"Bluster" in Spanish is "Estupido." :-D
Lobo

Lobo in English
is "mean boy."
:-(

Kaley Bluster

Date: Wednesday, November 29
To: by.the.sea@escuela.net.ve
From: Kaley@flutter.edu
Subject: NOT FUNNY

Dear Lobo,

Bluster is NOT "Estupido"!!!!!!!!!

I asked my teacher, and he told me what
"estupido" means. Not that I couldn't figure
it out for MYSELF, just by looking at the
word.

He also told me that many Spanish boy names usually end in
"o" and girl names end in "a." That gave me a great idea for
a nickname.

Happily,
Loba ☺

Kaley Bluster

Date: Wednesday, November 29
To: Kaley@flutter.edu
From: by.the.sea@escuela.net.ve
Subject: Your not-so-great idea

Hey,
"Loba" is estupida!
Quit copying.
Get your own nickname.
Didn't you ask if we could stop e-writing?
Let's.

#1 Lobo, the one and only ^..^

Loba is a fox!

Mr. Serrano,

I chose my second cyberpal from Zimbabwe since I recently learned how to spell it. Note: Zimbabwe is a <u>country</u> on the <u>continent</u> of Africa.

Yes, "Ley" was me. It was my nickname for 20 minutes—until Cal made up a song at recess that went, "Leyleyleyleyleyleyleyleyleyleyley" and just about drove me crazy.

Back to Kaley

Kaley Bluster

Date: Thursday, November 30
To: Zgrrl@harare.net.za
From: Kaley@flutter.edu
Subject: Looking for a cyberpal

Dear Muzwudzani,

Avuxeni from Los Estados Unidos!

Are you a girl or are you the opposite sex? I cannot tell by your name. My name (for now) is Kaley.

Do you have a nickname or do people call you Muzwudzani all the time? I am looking for a nickname, so if you have any good suggestions for "Kaley," let me know.

I'm supposed to ask about holidays in your country. Here, Thanksgiving is over and we are approaching Christmas, although you wouldn't know it by looking at my house because my parents think it's "too early to decorate." To me, August would not be too early.

Let me tell you about Christmas. In the middle of the night on December 24th, a large man in a red suit with a white beard flies across the sky in a sleigh full of gifts, pulled by reindeer.

When I type it out like that, it sounds pretty far-fetched. I wouldn't blame you if you didn't believe me. Do you celebrate Christmas in Zimbabwe?

Write and tell me about yourself.

Hoping you're a girl,
Kaley

P.S. I did not make up the part about flying reindeer.

Kaley Bluster

Date: Thursday, November 30
To: Kaley@flutter.edu
From: Zgrrl@harare.net.za
Subject: From my school to yours

Dear Kaley,

♪ Girls ♪
ROCK!
♪

Hello from Harare! Yes, I am a girl. You greeted me
in Tsonga, one of many languages in Zimbabwe.
(And you greeted me in Spanish. It is NOT one of the
languages here.)

Our official language is English. I did not know what
"nickname" meant until my teacher defined it. I have a
nickname. My friends call me Zani.

Yes, we celebrate Kisimusi (Christmas) in Zimbabwe.
My father works for a large hotel. A holiday meal
is prepared for the employees and families.
We dine on roasted ox and sing songs.
Afterwards, we go to church. When we get
home, my father surprises us with gifts.

LARGE
HOTEL

I have four older sisters who tease me because I am the
youngest. I think a brother would be more fun than sisters

who leave me out of their games. I would trade two of my sisters for one brother.

I like my school. I have been studying English since grade one, but I know words in Tsonga, Zulu, Venda, and Afrikaans. Do you study other languages at your school? Do you have brothers and sisters?

Yes, I have heard about flying reindeer.

I do not know a nickname for "Kaley." Perhaps a similar name would be "Kambo."

Sincerely,
Zani

Kaley Bluster

Date: Thursday, November 30
To: Zgrrl@harare.net.za
From: Kaley@flutter.edu
Subject: This is cool!

Dear Zani,

Brothers are not much fun. Trust me.
I have a baby brother you can borrow.
I wonder how much it would cost to
mail him to Zimbabwe?

I do not have sisters. I would be interested in trading, but not
if your sisters would tease me a lot and leave me out of their
games.

My school is Mildred Flutter Elementary. Apparently, people
aren't interested in who Mildred Flutter was. I guess that's
okay, because I'm not quite sure who she was either. All I
know is that she is dead and our school is named after her.
:-O

We do not learn a language until sixth grade. Unless you
consider English a language. Which it is. But I already know
it, so it doesn't count.

I'm thinking about "Kambo" as a nickname. I think the "nick" is supposed to be shorter than the "name." Kambo has the same number of letters as Kaley. But I'll give it a whirl.

Sincerely,
Kambo
(a.k.a. Kaley)

Kaley Bluster

Date: Thursday, November 30
To: Zgrrl@harare.net.za
From: Kaley@flutter.edu
Subject: NOT cool!

Dear Zani,

It's almost time for the dismissal bell, so I have to hurry and send this.

My class shares cyberpal news every afternoon before recess. A girl in my class named Shanay Wink heard about a new elephant at our zoo, and guess what its name is?

Kambo!!!

You do not want to know how horrible recess was for me. So much for the nickname. Thanks anyway. :'-<

Sincerely,
Kaley Again

4-get "Kambo"!
(Even though elephants never 4-get.)

Dear Kaley;

First, I am sorry the class laughed at you when Shanay told them about the elephant named Kambo.

Second, since you want people to know about Mildred Flutter, yet you have no idea who she was, I'll give you a head start on next week's essay assignment. Please write a biography of her life.

    Mr. Serrano

P.S. The "little heads" are called emoticons.

Mr. S,

My "head start on next week's essay" was spent looking through three sets of encyclopedias.

(Can I get extra credit for the extra work? Just in case, the three sets were: World Book, Collier's, and Grolier's.)

I did not find one word about Mildred.

K.

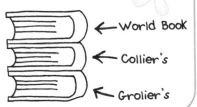

← World Book

← Collier's

← Grolier's

Kaley,

Try Googling "Mildred Flutter."

Mr. S.

Mr. S,

Googling? How can I
stare at a dead person?

Kaley, Konfused

Kaley,

Ask Ms. Bartholomew during
library time. She will show you
how to Google dead people to
learn about their lives. ☺

Mr. Serrano, Sighing

Books Ms. Bart
ordered for me:

✓ CASTLES AND YOU

✓ FAIRY TALE CASTLES

✓ IF YOU WERE A
  PRINCESS IN 1400

↑

She says this is a year,
not a room number.

December 4
Weekly Essay

Autobiography of Mildred Flutter
by Kaley Bluster

Thanks to the Googles, here is what I found:

Mildred Flutter was born a long, long, long, long time ago.

Her father, Mr. H. Bottom, was a general in the army, so Mildred grew up in Germany, Okinawa, and the Philippines.

My name is:
H. BOTTOM

I do not know what the "H." in "H. Bottom" stands for. Not "Harry," I hope.

Growing up overseas made Mildred want to travel the world. She visited nineteen countries—until her terrible accident.

It happened in Katmandu. What a weird and funny name.

The terrible accident involved a herd of nervous goats and a taxi in the middle of the monsoon season. I don't know why the goats were nervous. I don't know what "monsoon season" is either, but I am pretty sure we don't have it in this country since our seasons are known by other names.

(Note to Mr. S: For extra credit, the names of our seasons are: spring, summer, winter, and fall. Not necessarily in that order.)

When Mildred Bottom returned home to recover in the hospital, she married her doctor, Marvin Flutter. I'll bet she was glad to get rid of her maiden name. I'm glad, too, because I wouldn't want to tell people I go to Bottom Elementary.

After she married, Mildred considered combining her two last names into "Bottom-Flutter," but that sounded just plain weird, so she dropped her "Bottom" once and for all.

Mildred's husband called her Millie, so even *she* had a nickname. I think I will call her Millie for the rest of this essay.

Marvin + Millie 4 ever

Millie went to college at the Ida Wiggans School for Future Teachers. (Please don't ask who Ida Wiggans is because I do not want to write another essay. One a week is enough. And what if Ida Wiggans went to a school named after A. Nother Person? Then I'd have to write a biography of Mr. Person, too! This could go on until I graduate from Isaac C. Kazinski High School.)

(Ooops, I should not mention Isaac C. Kazinski since I don't know who he is either. Please be kind, Mr. S. I do not need to know who I.C.K. is until I get to high school.)

Back to the life of Mildred!

During college, Millie discovered her love of inventing things when she accidentally set a rubber lid on a hotplate in her dorm room. It melted into a shape that served perfectly as a window wedgie to hold the window open on warm days. The invention became known as "Millie's Wedgie."

Once the inventing bug bit, Millie went on to invent many other things. Sadly, she never got rich because none of her inventions caught on. (Good thing she married a doctor.)

inventing bug

Here is a list of her best unknown inventions.

1. Spoonife: combination of a spoon and a knife for quicker slicing and eating of fruit.

2. Bracelephone: telephone jewelry for secretaries.

3. Ear holster: for keeping pencils firmly tucked behind one ear.

4. Clockachore: a clock that chimes with reminders of things to do instead of the hour. (Note: I, Kaley Bluster, would never buy a clock that chimed "do your homework!" instead of "bong, bong, bong!")

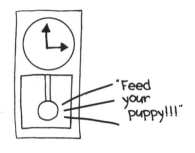

"Feed your puppy!!!"

You may be wondering how our school came to be named after Mildred Flutter. So was I, but Mr. Google did not know the answer. Ms. Bart told me I could find bits and pizzas of information about our "Founding Mother" on the local history shelf.

Here's what I found: The late Dr. Flutter owned the land our school is built on. (Note: Ms. Bart told me that "late" doesn't mean "tardy." It means "dead." I'm glad they call it the "tardy bell" when you're late to school and not the "dead bell." Triple ewww!)

Mildred planned to sell the land to the city for a garbage dump, but the Board of Education convinced her to donate the land so our school could be  built. In return, the school was named after her.

And now I understand what those weird things are in that old display case behind the globe stand in the library: a spoonife, bracelephone, ear holster, and clockachore. Oh, and a couple of wedgies.

THE END ☺

Dear Kaley,

Well, now we know more about our Founding Mother than we ever hoped—or needed—to know.

For the record, what you wrote was a "biography." Mildred's "autobiography" could only be written if she came back from the Great Beyond.

I am always open to student efforts toward extra credit. However, the information must <u>not</u> be "common knowledge," such as the names of the seasons or encyclopedias. So, no extra credit points this time. Sorry.

Please be careful about calling names "weird and funny." We are all encountering lots of different names during our cyberpal unit. Better to say a name is "memorable and intriguing."

You did focus on a few important pieces of information; however, attention to detail is a must for a good biography. In what year was Mildred Flutter born? You can do better than a "long, long, long, long time ago."

    Mr. Serrano

P.S. I believe the word is "wedge," not "wedgie." Look it up.

Mr. Serrano,

Mildred Flutter was born in 1930. Ms. Bart showed me those numbers listed after people's names in reference books. The numbers <u>before</u> the hyphen stand for the year they were born, and the ones <u>after</u> the hyphen represent the year they died.

I guess the trick is to leave the right side of the hyphen blank as long as you can.

Kaley

KALEY
1997—
4-ever

Ha ha ha!

Kaley Bluster

Date: Tuesday, December 5
To: Zgrrl@harare.net.za
From: Kaley@flutter.edu
Subject: Hello?? Avuxeni??

Dear Zani,

I have written to you twice and you haven't answered. We are supposed to be e-writing. Watz ^? :-Q

Worried,
Kaley

Write
me
right
back!

Kaley Bluster

Date: Tuesday, December 5
To: Kaley@flutter.edu
From: Zgrrl@harare.net.za
Subject: I'm here!!

Dear Kaley,

Sorry!

I have a new e-mail friend, and I have been quite busy
writing to her. She has her own Web site! On it are pictures
of her cats and games and jokes! It is so much fun to visit.
I think I will be cyberpals with her and not you.

Thank you for understanding,
Zani

P.S. My new friend's name is Shanay.
I think it is a pretty name.

Mr. Serrano!!!!

How come Shanay with her "memorable and intriguing" name has her own Web site? Can I get me one? Even though I have no cats or games or jokes?

Kaley

Kaley,

Shanay is using her home computer for extra credit on our cyberpal unit. If you are online at home, you can certainly set up a Web site of your own.

Mr. Serrano

Mr. S,

My dad says the last thing he wants to see after sitting at a computer all day is another one at home. BUT my mom wants a computer and so do I.

My dad said to ask Santa. I THINK it means we are getting one for Christmas. I hope hope hope so.

Cal is always playing games on Uncle Anthony's computer.
My uncle has his own Web site (how2getpubbed.com) to advertise his book on publishing, which no one wanted to publish. I'll ask him about Web sites—just in case Santa comes through.

K.

Kaley,

Ah, yes, I ran into your uncle at Stop and Go. Somehow, I ended up buying his book. Apparently, he keeps six boxes of them in his trunk for unsuspecting customers who really only wanted a quick loaf of bread.

Mr. S.

my computer
(I hope!!!)

Kaley Bluster

Date: Wednesday, December 6
To: marzipan@SaxonySchule.net.de
From: Kaley@flutter.edu
Subject: Introducing . . . . me!

Dear Ava,

Gluten morgan! My name is Kaley, and I picked your name from the cyberpal list because I just wrote a biography with the word "Germany" in it.

I am tired of writing the same things about my life so I'm attaching stuff I already wrote so you can get to know me.

Do you have your own Web site? I don't. I tried, but apparently it costs money, and my allowance is only five dollars a week. Do you get an allowance?

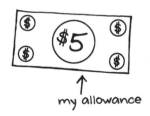

my allowance

My Uncle Anthony has a Web site. He told me I could take over one page and make it "Kaley's Korner."

I was really excited about having my own korner until I found out I'd have to write stuff, come up with games and jokes, and explode pictures. (. . . Maybe he said "upload" pictures. I can't remember. Not sure what it means.)

It all sounds like tooooo much work, even to show Shanay I can do it.

I was going to say "good-bye" in German, but I forgot how. Kaley

I ♡ dogs!

Kaley Bluster

Date: Wednesday, December 6
To: Kaley@flutter.edu
From: marzipan@SaxonySchule.net.de
Subject: hi from across the ocean

Dear Kaley,

"Good morning" in German is "GUTEN morgan," not gluten. Gluten is something you put into bread dough before you bake it. I know because my father owns a deli called "The Wurst of Bavaria."

Sometimes I help him make things. My favorites are candies, like pfefferminz and marzipan. You can probably translate the first one into English without my help, ja? And marzipan is candy made with lots of almonds and sugar. Delish!

I could not open your attachment. The school computer called it "spam" and would not let me open it. My father serves Spam in his deli. It is yummy, even if the computer does not like it.

When I go to the deli for lunch, I order bratwurst. It comes with mustard and a hard roll. I help him bake the rolls. (Yes, we add gluten to the dough!!!)

You asked if I get an allowance. I get "mad money" as my oma calls it. Ten euros a week.

Who is Shanay?
Good-bye in German is "auf wiedersehen."

Ava

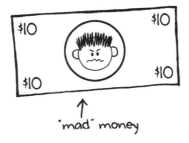

"mad" money

Kaley Bluster

Date: Wednesday, December 6
To: marzipan@SaxonySchule.net.de
From: Kaley@flutter.edu
Subject: Who told you?

Dear Ava,

How do you know about Shanay?
Did she write to you?
Did you go to her Web site?
What arc curos?
What are omas?
What is "ja"?

Auf grumpy,   l-(
Kaley

Kaley Bluster

Date: Wednesday, December 6
To: Kaley@flutter.edu
From: marzipan@SaxonySchule.net.de
Subject: Shanay

Dear Kaley,

I know about Shanay because you wrote about her. Does she have a Web site? Can I be her cyberpal?

Euros = money
Oma = my grandmother
Ja = yes

"Auf grumpy" is not a phrase, but it is funny and it made me laugh.

Auf hahaha,
Ava

Ha ha ha!

Kaley Bluster

Date: Wednesday, December 6
To: NahaTam@paaralan.net.jp
From: Kaley@flutter.edu
Subject: From your new cyberpal

Dear Tamaki,

My name is Kaley, and I picked your name from the cyberpal list because I just wrote a biography with "Okinawa" in it.

Please write back. I need to find lots of cyberpals because Shanay keeps taking them away from me.

Do you have a nickname?

Hoping this one works,
Kaley

Kaley Bluster

Date: Wednesday, December 6
To: Kaley@flutter.edu
From: NahaTam@paaralan.net.jp
Subject: helloooo over there!

Dear Kaley,

Haisai from Okinawa! Sometimes my friends call me Tam
rather than Tamaki. Is that what you mean by "nickname"?

I live in the city of Naha, where the weather is
sunny and hot all year, even though we are close
to Japan, where it snows in the winter.

Okinawa is a large island. My school teaches in English, but I
also speak Japanese. I will teach you how to count to five:

ichi
ni
san
shi
go

↖ I found these on
a Web site

One of my favorite things to do is visit the castle of the Sho
Dynasty. Do you have castles in America?

My favorite food is andagi. They are like donuts.

I take karate and am the best in my class.
I am ichiban! (Number one!) Did you
know that karate originated in Okinawa?
Do you know karate?

Sincerely,
Tamaki or Tam

P.S. Who is Shanay and why is she stealing your cyberpals?

Kaley Bluster

Date: Thursday, December 7
To: NahaTam@paaralan.net.jp
From: Kaley@flutter.edu
Subject: Back atcha

Dear Tamaki or Tam,

My cousin Cal does karate. He's always trying it out on me, so I've learned a few hollers and kicks. He taught me how to do the roundhouse kick and then got mad when I used it on him. Hrgh! (←the holler) (Cal hates it when I call them hollers. He says they're called "spirit yells.")

Thank you for teaching me how to count in Japanese. I hope I can use it for extra credit since it is not "common knowledge."

I told Shanay I was "number ichi," and she reported it to the school nurse, who made me stay in during recess "for observation," then sent me back to class with six packets of anti-itch lotion.

I love castles, too, so we have something in common!!! I don't know if we have castles in America or not. Maybe the

White House in Washington, D.C. I'm not sure.

I looove castles!

Do you know any Japanese nicknames for Kaley?

Meanwhile, I'm so excited because we FINALLY put up our Christmas tree last night!

I wanted a real tree. My dad promises us one every year, but the weather always turns icy cold just when it's time to go looking, and no one wants to tromp around tree farms in the snow except me.

the Bluster family Christmas tree

In protest, I refused to come out of my room while Dad set up the metal tree. Not even for Grandma Bluster's peanut brittle. Metal trees are unnatural. One, because they're METAL, not FUR, and two, because this one is WHITE. Whoever heard of a white Christmas tree? (Unless it snows, but I don't think it's going to snow in the middle of our living room anytime soon.)

My mom sprayed evergreen scent all over the house to make me feel better, but it only gave Cal an asthma attack. (Cal was here, helping.) He had to run outside (in the icy cold) and use his inhaler.

My mom felt horrible and terrible and awful, all at the same time. She opened all the windows to air out the house, then taught Cal yoga breathing to clear his lungs and balance his chi. (I don't know what his chi is or why it needed balancing, but it was funny to watch.)

All the icy air whooshed inside, so we put on our winter coats. My dad gave this huge sigh and said, "Since we're already freezing and bundled up tight, we might as well drive to the tree farm and be miserable." Cal and I jumped around the room, cheering and double-high-fiving in our gloves. ^5 ^5

Boy, that yoga breathing and chi balancing worked fast.

So, off we went to the tree farm and brought home a real, live, naturally green fur. Apparently, Cal is not allergic to real trees—only to sprays that smell like real trees.

We drank eggnog as we decorated. It was fun, except Cal broke the bread dough angel I made in second grade. I wonder if the angel had gluten in her.

Sayonara! (←Ms. Bart in the library wrote this down for me. I think it means "good-bye" in Japanese.)

Kaley

Kaley,

Remember our unit on homophones? It's <u>fir</u> tree, not <u>fur</u>, although the latter makes an interesting image!

Mr. S.

P.S. I'm glad Cal is okay.

Kaley Bluster

Date: Thursday, December 7
To: Dak@ManilaAcademy.net.ph
From: Kaley@flutter.edu
Subject: Willing to be a cyberpal?

Dear Dakila,

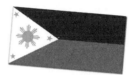

Halo from the United States! My name is
Kaley, and I picked you from the cyberpal
list because I just wrote a biography with
"Philippines" in it.

Tell me about you first. Then I'll tell you about me.

Do people call you Dakila or do you have a nickname? Is
there a nickname in your country for "Kaley?" If so, please
let me know.

Adiyos! (which looks a lot like good-bye in Spanish: adios)
(But if you're ever in Venezuela, say "chow" instead of "adios,"
even though they speak Spanish there. Don't ask me why.)

Kaley

Kaley,

Just a reminder: When you begin e-writing with a new cyberpal, you have to keep it up until it mutually ends. Be careful not to overextend yourself!

Since you seem so obsessed with nicknames—as well as earning extra credit points—give me 300 words on "The Origin of Names."

"Nick" (my nickname)
(Mr. S.)

(Now you've got _me_ overusing parentheses. . . .)

December 8
Extra Credit (triple yay!)

Where Do Names Come From?
by Kaley Bluster

Although the rest of the class spent study time writing to their cyberpals, I spent mine writing an essay for extra credit. (Even though I offered to count to five in Japanese for the same amount of extra credit—which would have been a lot faster.)

(Is your nickname really "Nick," or are you teasing me? That's like saying your pen name is "Pen.")

About names . . .

Names go back as far as the very first people on Earth, because they had to call each other something to keep everyone straight.

All we can do is guess at these early names. They probably had something to do with the way a person looked (Shorty) or smelled (Stinky) or talked (Og the Loud).

As years passed, names became more descriptive: Og the Brave, Og the Foolish, or Og the Late. (In this case, "late" means "late," and not "dead," albeit they didn't have clocks back then, so being late was not invented until much later.)

Names were also used to describe a person's relationship to his father. The son of Og would be Ogson. No one knows what Og's daughter was called since Ogsdaughter sounds estupido.

The name Og was very popular in the beginning, but soon fell off the top-ten list. People started using jobs to describe each other.

The man who wove cloth became "Weaver." The man who made bread was "Baker." And two guys named "Barnes" and "Noble" started selling books.

If the same rule applied today, Mr. Serrano's name might be "Teacher." Or "Teacherson" if his father had been a teacher, too.

As even more years passed, some people were described by phrases: "Benoni" means "son of my sorrow." "Matthew" means "brother who was supposed to be a sister." "Shanay" means "I have a Web site and you don't." This is my favorite way of naming people.

Sometimes people combined two words that described a person: "Victorybattle" (a soldier), "Peaceflower" (not a soldier), or "Starbucks" (a coffee maker).

"star" bucks

Soon, so many people had similar names they had to invent "sirnames" (like "Sir Speedy.") After that, last names were invented. These usually told where someone lived. The man with the beard by the hill might be "Redbeard de la Mound." The nosy lady who lived by a bank might be "Gossip de la Money."

Soon, nicknames were invented to save time and to sound cool. The man who tended geese by the lake became "Goose," even though his real name was "Bird Man de la Large Body of Water."

And guess what? I came up with a nickname for Baby Matthew: Mattie!!!! My dad says he won't like it when he gets old enough to protest. But when I call him "Mattie," he grins like he's soooooo happy to have a nickname this early in life.

I just wish he would grow some teeth so his grins looked better.

Back to names!

Some names are too short to turn into a nickname. All the Ogs stayed Og for as long as they lived.

I have gone over 300 words so I am done.

Kaley de la Finished

Og's dog

To Kaley the Clever,

Actually, the ending "daughter of" is used in Scandinavia and is spelled "dottir."
Also, I believe you mean "surnames," not "sirnames."

Yes, Nick is really my nickname. Short for Nicholas. (As in <u>Saint</u> Nicholas—a title I feel I am slowly earning. . . .)

Mattie is a good nickname for your brother. At least until he learns how to talk back.

Good job on the essay; however, the last paragraph should wrap up your final thoughts, not be a comment on how many words you have written. If you can give me a better ending, I'll give you your extra credit points.

Mr. Serrano

P.S. By the way, I want to see you and Shanay after school.

Where Do Names Come From?
Rewrite of ending
by Kaley Blusterdottir

Once names were invented, they never went out of fashion, which is why we still have names to this day. Some of us even have cool nicknames. (Like the one I made up for my brother!)

The End. Again.

Kaley,

Thank you for the thoughtful revision of your ending.

Mr. Grateful That the Weekend Is Here

Mr. Serrano,

On Friday, when Shanay and I stayed after school, I'm sorry I "wasn't very pleasant." (What my Grandma Bluster calls it.) I just didn't feel like talking.

Shanay acts like everything she does is so wonderful—like bragging about her cyberpal in Hamsterdam. I'll bet there's no such place. I think hamsters live all over the world.

Cal used to have a hamster until it disappeared inside his mom's closet. Aunt Phoebe wore the same clothes for a week until Uncle Anthony convinced her that the hamster was long gone. Cal never found it. Unfortunately, his mom did. (Three months later in her snow boot, in case you were wondering.) (It was dead.) (We had a funeral for the hamster _and_ the boot, but I'll tell you about that some other time.)

Any chance of moving Shanay to the other fourth grade? I think that would solve my problem.

Kaley

Kaley,

Apology accepted. No to your request. You and Shanay need to work things out between you.

    Mr. Serrano

P.S. It's Amsterdam, not Hamsterdam, which, again, makes for an interesting image. . . .

"interesting image" of Cal's hamster

R.I.P.

Kaley Bluster

Date: Monday, December 11
To: Kaley@flutter.edu
From: marzipan@SaxonySchule.net.de
Subject: knock, knock . . .

Dear Kaley,

You did not write back! I thought we were cyberpals, ja?

We are celebrating Weihnachten (Christmas) in our class.
Today was my turn to bring treats. My father baked
baumkuchen at his deli. I sprinkled on powdered sugar after
he topped the cake with apricot jam. Yummy!

Fröhliches Weihnachten!
(Merry Christmas)
Ava

Kaley Bluster

Date: Monday, December 11
To: Kaley@flutter.edu
From: NahaTam@paaralan.net.jp
Subject: Answers from Okinawa

Dear Kaley,

Funny joke about the itch (ichi) cream!

Yes, "sayonara" is "good-bye" in Japanese.
It was also the name of an old movie, but
I have never seen it. My grandmother saw
it many times, because she had a crush
on an actor named Marlon Brando in the
movie. I have never heard of him.

Marlon
Brando
WHO?

I could not think of a Japanese nickname for "Kaley." Sorry.

In karate, we are learning "mokuso" (meditation). It is
difficult for me to sit still with my eyes closed, but
I do it so my sensei (teacher) will be proud of me.

Write soon!
Tamaki

Kaley Bluster

Date: Monday, December 11
To: Kaley@flutter.edu
From: Dak@ManilaAcademy.net.ph
Subject: All about Dakila—that's me!

Dear Kaley,

Hello from the Philippines! Thank you for writing. You did not tell me anything about yourself except that you wanted a nickname. I do not have one. Everyone calls me Dakila all the time. I think the closest Filipino name to yours would be "Kaya."

My family owns a coconut farm outside of the city. My school is in Manila, so I live in a dorm during the week and go home on weekends. I travel back and forth with my two brothers.

farmer

Classes are taught in English. You greeted me (Halo) in Tagalog, one of fifty-five languages spoken in different parts of our country. Some of the other languages are: Waray-waray, Pangasinan, and Bicolano. I know a few words from many languages, but Tagalog is mostly spoken in Manila.

Now tell me about you and the USA. Is English spoken everywhere, or do you have different languages in different parts of your country?

Masaya Pasko!
(Merry Christmas)
Dakila

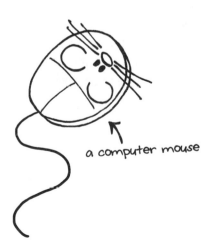

a computer mouse

Kaley Bluster

Date: Monday, December 11
To: marzipan@SaxonySchule.net.de
From: Kaley@flutter.edu
Subject: Holiday treats

Dear Ava,

We bring treats to class, too. I wanted to bring
Grandma Bluster's peanut brittle, but Cal ate it all.
(I called my grandma "oma," and she told me not to sass.
I don't think she knows I can speak other languages.)

My mother used to make star cookies with icing and red
sprinkles, but that was before Mattie was born. (Mattie is my
brother Matthew's nickname.) (I made it up.) Last Thursday
was my turn to bring treats. I had to bring Keebler's. I
dumped out the cookies and buried the package in the trash.
Still, kids knew. Embarrassing!

Kaley

Kaley Bluster

Date: Monday, December 11
To: NahaTam@paaralan.net.jp
From: Kaley@flutter.edu
Subject: Hi karate ☺

Dear Tamaki,

I am tired of Cal leaping out at me and hollering karate words I don't understand. Can you teach him mokuso? I would like it if he sat still with his eyes closed for long periods of time.

Kaley

Kaley Bluster

Date: Monday, December 11
To: Dak@ManilaAcademy.net.ph
From: Kaley@flutter.edu
Subject: Our language

Dear Dakila,

"Tagalog" is a . . . "memorable and intriguing" name for a language. (I didn't know they named languages after Girl Scout cookies!)

Yes, English is spoken all over the USA.

Wait. So is Spanish. I hear it all the time.

Tagalogs . . .
YUM!!

Come to think of it, my friend's grandparents speak Yiddish. The ladies at the place Grandma Bluster gets her hair dyed speak Vietnamese. And the butcher my mom goes to is from Pakistan, and he taught me how to say "hello" in Punjabi: "namaste." My mother already knew how to say it because she uses "namaste" in her yoga classes.

So I guess there ARE a lot of languages spoken in the USA. I'd never really thought about it.

I like "Kaya" as a nickname for Kaley. Guess I'll try it out.

Kaya

P.S. No disrespect, but I do not like coconut. Not even drowned in 50 layers of chocolate.

YUCK!!

Kaley Bluster

Date: Tuesday, December 12
To: Kaley@flutter.edu
From: Zgrrl@Harare.net.za
Subject: Me again

Dear Kaley,

Remember me? Zani from Zimbabwe?
Just wanted to tell you that Shanay wrote
something mean about you on her Web site
blog. She wrote that your nickname is
what crows say when they land in a corn
patch . . . Kaya! Kaya! :-@

I did not like it, so I stopped writing to her. I can
be cyberpals with you again if you still want to!

Zani

P.S. My sister's friend's cousin's grandma's godson has an
aunt named "Kaisy." Would you want that for a nickname?

Kaley Bluster

Date: Tuesday, December 12
To: Zgrrl@Harare.net.za
From: Kaley@flutter.edu
Subject: Yes, let's be cyberpals again

Dear Zani,

Thank you for telling me what Shanay wrote. Now I understand what my teacher meant when he asked Shanay to stop blogging during our Letter Writing unit. I thought he meant for her to stop bragging. (I think she should stop doing that, too.)

I like "Kaisy." It's triple cool. But picking a nickname that rhymes with "crazy" is asking to be tortured by certain people during recess. Thanks anyway. :~/

Sadly,
Kaley Once More

Mr. Serrano!!!!

I know it's only December 13th, but last night after dinner, my dad surprised my mom and me with a big box wrapped in glittery paper. We tore it open and guess what? It was a computer! Now I can host my very own "Kaley's Korner" Web site.

My dad set it up in the basement on his old desk from college. He showed me how to e-mail from home and bug Cal electronically even though I bug him in person every day. Triple fun!

Well, I just thought you'd want to know that I plan on making lots of extra credit points with my home computer, just like Shanay.

Kaley

P.S. Mattie thought the glittery paper was the gift—not what was inside.

Kaley,

Glad to hear Santa came a week and a half early! Enjoy playing with your new "toy." Why not ask Shanay for tips on how to set up your own Web site?

Mr. S.

Kaley Bluster

Date: Wednesday, December 13
To: Kaley@flutter.edu
From: marzipan@SaxonySchule.net.de
Subject: Holiday programs

Dear Kaley,

My class is conducting a play. Pinocchio.
I get to be a dancing rag doll. What does
your class do for the holidays?

Ava

Pinocchio's
nose

Kaley Bluster

Date: Wednesday, December 13
To: Kaley@flutter.edu
From: NahaTam@paaralan.net.jp
Subject: Traditions?

Dear Kaley,

Please tell me what schools in the USA do to celebrate your holiday season.

Tamaki

Kaley Bluster

Date: Wednesday, December 13
To: Kaley@flutter.edu
From: Dak@ManilaAcademy.net.ph
Subject: What's cold weather like?

Dear Kaley,

I listen to American holiday music and can't imagine cold weather, falling snow, skating on ice, and wearing coats. Here, it is warm all the time. People put holiday lights in palm trees. What is it like at your school this time of year?

Dakila

Kaley Bluster

Date: Wednesday, December 13
To: Kaley@flutter.edu
From: Zgrrl@Harare.net.za
Subject: Glad you're not mad!

Dear Kaley,

I am happy to be cyberpals again. Tell me what your class is doing for the holidays.

Zani

Kaley Bluster

Date: Wednesday, December 13

To: marzipan@SaxonySchule.net.de

             NahaTam@paaralan.net.jp

             Dak@ManilaAcademy.net.ph

             Zgrrl@Harare.net.za

From: Kaley@flutter.edu

Subject: Our Class Play

Dear Ava, Tamaki, Dakila, and Zani,

I know it's against the rules to send a group e-mail. (Sorry, Mr. S, but I'll never get my final essay written if I have to keep answering e-mail.) :{ :{ :{

You all asked how we celebrate the holidays in my class. I will tell you!

The entire fourth grade is putting on a play. And guess what? My uncle Anthony wrote it! (My uncle says he is a famous author minus the famous part.)

School rules say that the program cannot have anything to do with Christmas, Hanukkah, Kwanza, or even Santa. Not one elf or reindeer can appear. I think trees are okay, but they can't have ornaments. And no angels!!! (Which makes me sad, because I always wanted to play an angel and wear a sparkly halo and wings—even though Cal says I'm not "angel material.")

sad angel

Uncle Anthony's script is about a dog named "Bob," who is trying to find a happy home before the cold of winter. My uncle wanted Bob to be chased by "Jack Frost," but Mr. Serrano was afraid Jack might be on the school's "no-no" list. (Mr. S. says Jack Frost "disappears every year between March and September, which some folks might find highly suspicious.") (I think he was joking.)

I play an innkeeper with a "no dogs allowed" policy at my inn, so I have to turn Bob away.

Shanay gets to play a princess in a castle. Bob wants to make it his happy home, but the princess keeps cats, so Bob is not welcome. (Shanay wants to bring her cats to school the day of the play, but my teacher said no.) (Yay!)

I thought I should be chosen to play the princess, because my teacher knows how much I love castles. Shanay gets to wear her hair swooped up under a tall, pointy hat with a veil, and I "get" to wear a nametag that says "The Bluster Inn." Ho hum. Not fair.

Cal gets to play the hero who finally gives Bob a happy home. I'll bet he got the part because his dad wrote the play. (A GIRL could just as well be the hero who takes Bob in.)

The BEST part of the program is that the role of "Bob" will be played by King, the puppy Mr. Serrano adopted from the batch Ms. Bartholomew had. (I don't mean Ms. Bart had the batch of puppies. Her dog did.)

King Bob

And here's the most important part of all. Guess who is responsible for Mr. S. adopting King? ME!!!!!

Since I am the one who found "King Bob" for Mr. Serrano, it only seems fair for me to play the princess hero who gives Bob a happy home.

Princess Kaley

And that's how the fourth grade at Mildred Flutter Elementary is celebrating Christmas—I mean, the Holidays.

Before I sign off . . . if any of you have e-mail at home and want to keep e-talking after our cyberpal unit is over, you can write to me at: KB@home.com.

Felix Navidad! (I borrowed that from Shanay's cyberpal in Argentina. It means Merry Christmas in Spanish. There's supposed to be an upside-down exclamation point at the beginning, but I can't make one with this keyboard.)

Kaley

Kaley;

You're right; it's against the rules to send a group e-mail. Ten points will come off your grade. Please follow the rules.

You were there when all the parts in the play were drawn out of a hat, so you can't say it wasn't fair.

It's Feli_z_ Navidad. Feli_x_ is a cat.

It's a _litter_ of puppies, not a batch.

And a girl hero is called a _heroine_.

Mr. "Only-3 More Days Till Winter Break" Serrano

Kaley Bluster

Date: Wednesday, December 13
To: KATLUV@Shanay.webnet
From: KB@home.com
Subject: Questions about Web sites

Hi Shanay,

I visited your Web site tonight and found your home e-mail
address. Questions:
1. How did you find your own korner of the Internet?
2. How did you put pictures on your page?
3. Was it hard to find the jokes and games?

Thanks,
Kaley (from school)

Kaley Bluster

Date: Wednesday, December 13
To: KB@home.com
From: KATLUV@Shanay.webnet
Subject: U & UR ?s

Y shud I hlp U?
U told Zani 2 stop CPing w/me.
WEG~

Sh'nay

Kaley, Konfused

HUH?

???

Kaley Bluster

Date: Wednesday, December 13
To: by.the.sea@escuela.net.ve
From: KB@home.com
Subject: Need help translating

Hi Lobo,

It's Kaley, remember me? I'm e-mailing you from home on Wednesday night. Can you please look at the message below and tell me what it means?

> From: KATLUV@Shanay.webnet
> Subject: U & UR ?s
>
> Y shud I hlp U?
> U told Zani 2 stop CPing w/me.
> WEG~
>
> Sh'nay

Thank you,
Kaley

P.S. Would you believe I STILL haven't found a nickname? :-}

Kaley Bluster

Date: Thursday, December 14
To: KB@home.com
From: by.the.sea@escuela.net.ve
Subject: Helping the newbie
cc: Kaley@flutter.edu

WEG

Hey,
Found your message this morning.
Can't do personal mail at school.
E-mail at home: wolfboy@ventana.net.ve
Translation:
U & UR ?s = you and your questions
Y shud I hlp U? = why should I help you?
U told Zani 2 stop CPing w/me = (surely, you got THIS line? 2EZ)
WEG = wicked evil grin
Who is Sh'nay? She sounds cool.
FAB Web site.
hwga
(I'll translate now so you don't keep bugging me:
hwga = here we go again)
Lobo   ^..^

Kaley Bluster

Date: Thursday, December 14

To: wolfboy@ventana.net.ve

From: Kaley@flutter.edu

Subject: Gracias (←new word I just learned from
               Mr. S!)

Lobo,

Thanks (gracias) for your help, even though you think I'm
bugging you. (You sound like Cal.) I suspected Shanay's
weird letters and numbers weren't answering my questions.
I'll try again 2nite at home. (←see? I can do it, 2) :)

Kaley, who is guessing "CPing" means "cyberpal-ing."

CHICKS
RULE!

December 14
Final Essay
Letter Writing Sub-unit on E-mail

Topic: Give an overview of your experience with your cyberpal(s), including "the good, the bad, the spam." Tell what you learned from communicating with friends in other countries.

Cyberpals (According to Kaley)
by Kaley Bluster

Writing to new friends in other countries was fun and not-fun at the same time.

My first cyberpal, Lobo (^..^), did not want to e-write with me (the bad) but gave me the idea of getting my own nickname (the good— even though the "good" part hasn't happened yet.) And Ava told me that spam is eaten in Germany. I don't know how they do that.

I have to hurry and finish this essay because tomorrow is dress rehearsal for our program, and I'm not ready. We had to learn all of our lines by yesterday, which was easy for me since I have only <u>one</u> line: "Alas, you cannot live here, Bob, because no dogs are allowed at the Bluster Inn." (Yawn.)

I'm still figuring out my costume. I want to wear one of my dad's ties. There are so many of them dumped in his car, it will be hard to choose just one.

Back to cyberpals!

Some of them make you think they are foreigners, and then you find out they were born in the USA, so there's nothing you can tell them that they don't already know. Some cyberpals have names that force you to guess if they are girls or boys. (Note: They do not like it when you guess wrong.)

Most kids speak all sorts of languages, including English. (I learned bits and pizzas of Spanish, Japanese, German, Zimbab-wean, and Philippine-nean.)

Some kids have looooong names like Muzwudzani, yet find cool nicknames like Zani— and uncool nicknames like something you'd call an elephant. If you run into an elephant in Zimbabwe, you would greet him with "halo!" and give him "andiggies" (or whatever Okinawa donuts are called. I forget.).

If the elephant threatens you, offer him a coconut from your farm or use a karate holler on him, unless you are practicing "mokuso"—then you'd better stop meditating and RUN LIKE CRAZY.

Cal just delivered my "inn" for the play. It's a piece of tag board with a door and windows drawn on it. (Drawn badly, I must say. Cal is <u>not</u> a good draw-er and should not be in charge of scenery.)

I wish I could fancy up my inn. Maybe I can find out how to spell "The Bluster Inn" in Tagalog and decorate the door with pictures of Girl Scout cookies.

BRB.

Back.

(Mr. S.—Sorry for being at a computer when I'm supposed to be at my desk finishing my essay, but I thought it was okay to <u>research</u> our essays so we get the <u>facts</u> right.)

Back to cyberpals!

They live in Venezuela (a former CP, I mean), Zimbabwe (a former CP, who got mad at Shanay and came back to e-write with me), Germany, Okinawa, and the Philippines.

I learned how to say hello in Tsonga, count to five in Japanese, and say good-bye in German. (I'd give examples, but I don't remember how to spell any of the words.) (Unless you'd consider giving me extra credit for going back and looking them up.) (Let me know.)

I learned that Web sites are very useful for attracting cyberpals, but not if you don't know how to set one up or explode pictures of cute, fluffy kittens.

Finally, I learned that bread is made from gluten in the morgan.

This is the end of my essay because I have to go check my e-mail to see if my RESEARCH question was answered.

THE END ☺

Kaley Bluster

Date: Thursday, December 14
To: KATLUV@Shanay.webnet
From: KB@home.com
Subject: U did it 1st

You took Zani away from me last week. I didn't make her stop CPing with you. She didn't like it when you made fun of me in your blog, and that's the truth. Why DID you make fun of me? And why won't you answer my questions about Web sites?

K'ley

Web site???

LOL!

Kaley Bluster

Date: Thursday, December 14
To: KB@home.com
From: KATLUV@Shanay.webnet
Subject: DGT!!!!

Lobo warned me I'd have to explain e-slang to U.

DGT means DON'T GO THERE. What THAT means is . . . don't U dare start writing your name K'ley. Stop being a copycat.

I didn't make fun of U in my blog. I made fun of the stooopid nicknames U keep coming up with. Lobo told me U tried to copy him, too. What's wrong with just plain Kaley?

I'm Shanay at school, but at home, I'm Sh'nay. You can be anything you want at home. Just be original and stop stealing ideas.

Sh'nay

Kaley Bluster

Date: Thursday, December 14
To: KATLUV@Shanay.webnet
From: KB@home.com
Subject: How did you get Lobo's address???

See? You're stealing my cyberpals again. I found Lobo first.

I'm sorry I e-mailed you. I just thought you could tell me how you got your Web site and how you set it up. Mr. Serrano TOLD me to ask you.

KB (←me, at home—or at least at home.com)

Kaley Bluster

Date: Thursday, December 14
To: KB@home.com
From: KATLUV@Shanay.webnet
Subject: ^..^ boy

Lobo e-mailed me because U left my addy on when you cut and pasted my message to him. He's kewl.

The reason I don't want to help U set up your own site: you'll get bunches of extra credit from Mr. Serrano. You **always** do, and you always get a better grade on our units. This time, **I** want to be the best.

attt (and that's the truth)

Sh'nay

Shanay's "wink"

Kaley Bluster

Date: Thursday, December 14
To: KATLUV@Shanay.webnet
From: KB@home.com
Subject: Not fair!

You can't be the only one who gets extra credit for putting
cool stuff on a Web site.

KB

My name is: *Kaley*
Kaley
Kaley
Kaley ← I like this one best ☺

Kaley Bluster

Date: Thursday, December 14
To: KB@home.com
From: KATLUV@Shanay.webnet
Subject: Can2 nmi

For stooopid cluebies:
nmi means "no message inside" so there was no reason 4 U to open this e-mail. Gotcha!

Sh'nay

Kaley Bluster

Date: Thursday, December 14
To: KATLUV@Shanay.webnet
From: KB@home.com
Subject: But there WAS a message inside so don't
call ME stooopid nmi

who's stooopid now?

Kaley Bluster

Date: Thursday, December 14
To: KB@home.com
From: KATLUV@Shanay.webnet
Subject: U don't get it

It's not just cool stuff on my Web site. Mr. Serrano said it had to be additional info about 1 of my cyberpal countries, so I added factoids about India, thanks to my cyberpal in New Deli.

It's a LOT of xtra work. U couldn't do it because U aren't Web savvy, like ME. ☺☺☺☺

Well, I have to go try on my kewl princess costume for tomorrow's dress rehearsal.

Don't forget to try on your nametag. LOL!

Sh'nay

Kaley Bluster

Date: Thursday, December 14
To: KATLUV@Shanay.webnet
From: KB@home.com
Subject: IHUTOYPVAMYL

In case you peek to see that **I** know e-lingo, too, the subject line stands for: I hope you trip on your princess veil and muff your lines.

I don't believe there's any such place as New Deli. (One of my cyberpals, Ava, practically lives in her father's deli, and she would have mentioned knowing of a city with the same name.)

And I can be Web savvy, 2. Just W8&C. (←do I need to translate this 4 U?)

KB

Kaley Bluster

Date: Thursday, December 14
To: KATLUV@Shanay.webnet
From: KB@home.com
Subject: < No Subject >

Dear Shanay,

I didn't hear my dad come down the basement steps, so I did NOT know he was reading over my shoulder. He is making me write back to say I am sorry for being mean. And he grounded me from cyberspace at home. I'm not allowed to use the new computer until way after Christmas. ☹☹☹

Now he's making me say something nice to you. So . . . see you at school tomorrow. I hope dress rehearsal goes well. Break a leg! (Don't get mad at ME for that. My dad told me it's what you're supposed to say to actors in a play.)

Merry Christmas,
Kaley Bluster

broken leg

Kaley Bluster

Date: Saturday, December 16
To: CubsFan@hoptoad.com
From: Jbluster@acme.net
Subject: It's me, Kaley!

Dear Mr. Serrano (Mr. CubsFan ☺),

I am a fan of this cub!

Ms. Bart gave me your home e-mail address so I could write to you over the weekend. My dad is letting me "entertain myself" on his office computer. He needed to finish up some work in the shiny-window building, so I rode along.

I know you'll be at school on Monday for our program, but I couldn't wait to find out how King is doing after what happened at yesterday's dress rehearsal.

I'm sorry sorry sorry the puppy ran out the gym door. And I'm sorry I didn't notice right away after promising I'd keep an eye on him until it was time for his part in the program. I was too busy writing a new name for my inn on the tag board with a berry-colored marker and cutting out pictures of Girl Scout cookies from a scouting magazine.

Girl Scout cookies

Here's what happened: Shanay found a button on the floor by the door, and I recognized it from the costume King wears as "Bob." I went to look for him, and Shanay followed—which was a surprise because she's mad at me.

I'm mad at her, too, in case you were wondering. But when we realized the puppy had run away, we became so worried about him, we ran right out the door without stopping to get our coats, even though it was snowing.

King in costume ←

When we found King caught on the fence by the hood of his traveling cape, it took both of us to get him loose. Remember when you said you wished Shanay and I could get along better? Well, you should have seen us! I was so upset when I heard the puppy whimpering, I forgot to be mad at Shanay. I guess she forgot, too, because she worked and worked to get King's cape unhooked from the fence. My hands were shaking, so I'm glad she was there to do it. The ties of the cape had gotten tangled in King's collar, and we couldn't get the cape or the collar off of him.

While Shanay untangled, I held onto King and sang "Jingle Bells" in his ear real soft to keep him calm. I hope I didn't break any rules by singing a Christmas song on school grounds.

When we walked back to the building, I let Shanay carry King, even though I really wanted to. (That pouty-sad look works!)

Shanay told me she didn't mean to steal my cyberpal from Zimbabwe. She said her mother worked there for two years with the Peas Core. (????) She promised her mom she'd try to find a cyberpal from that country.

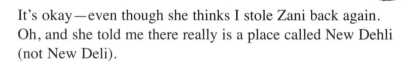

It's okay—even though she thinks I stole Zani back again. Oh, and she told me there really is a place called New Dehli (not New Deli).

After that, Shanay told me how easy it is to set up a free Web site. One of the games on her site is called "Name Generator," and she thought it might help me find a good nickname. I'm going over to Cal's tonight, and we're both going to try it on Uncle Anthony's computer. (I'm already grounded from using MY new computer. Don't ask.)

Well, my dad is ready to leave, so I'll "sign off," as he calls it. By the way, I asked him what he does here in his office with all the shiny windows. He said his job consists of three important tasks:

    1. (ichi) Crunching numbers
    2. (ni)   Shuffling papers
    3. (san) Scrolling and clicking

I'm glad I finally found out about the important work he does all day while I'm at school, albeit I still don't understand what it means or why he needs to wear a tie to do it.

That's all, Mr. S. I hope to hear that King (Bob) is okay and that the cuts and scratches from the fence weren't too bad. If you write back, please send your e-mail to Cal's address (KarateCal@home.com) since I'll be there tonight and . . . did I mention I can't use my OWN computer again until January?

Kaley

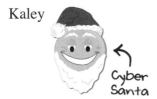

Cyber
Santa

Kaley Bluster

Date: Saturday, December 16
To: KarateCal@home.net
From: CubsFan@hoptoad.com
Subject: Message for Kaley!

Kaley!

What a surprise to find your message on my home computer.

animal doctor

I appreciate your concern for King. The vet kept him overnight. I just brought him home. The doc patched up all of King's scrapes and told me to keep him warm and well-fed over the weekend. She said he would be as good as new for his big stage debut on Monday.

Glad you and Shanay were such quick thinkers. You figured out where King had run off to, then overcame your differences and worked together to rescue him. I'm proud of you both. Don't know what I'd do if King had run away. I've gotten rather attached to the scruffy guy—thanks to you.

See you on Monday.

Mr. Serrano, with a pile of essays to grade and a sleeping pup to keep him company.

P.S. I know it's Saturday and you should get a day off from being corrected by your teacher, but I couldn't let this one slip past: It's the PEACE CORPS.

Kaley,

You did a very good job in the play today. Excellent projection of your voice and enunciation of your line.

At first, I was confused by the name change of your inn (and the cookie art). But after you explained that "Ang Bluster Bahay-Tuluyan" is "The Bluster Inn" in Tagalog (and Ms. Bart explained the Girl Scout connection—although she said the cookies are actually called "Tagalongs."), I was SO impressed that I gave you 15 extra credit points.

Super job!

I liked your plan to "help" Bob on his journey by walking him to each of his potential happy homes. It gave you a much bigger part in the play.

Putting King on a leash kept me from worrying about him running away again since lots of people were going in and out the gym doors.

(Very creative of you to make a dog leash out of your father's ties. I hope he doesn't mind.)

As for your final essay . . . after winter break, we'll have to talk about how to "stay on topic"—although, if you do, grading papers won't be nearly as challenging.

Mr. Serrano

P.S. It's "bits and PIECES," not pizzas. Look it up. (But not till after winter break.)

Letter Writing
Email Sub-unit with Cyberpals
Student: Kaley Bluster

Grades:
Following directions: C+
Interaction with cyberpal(s): B
Final Essay with extra credit points: B+
Keeping your teacher entertained: A

Nice work!

Mr. Serrano,

I couldn't leave for winter break without telling you what the name generator on Shanay's Web site told Cal and me.

First, Bob is actually a nickname for "Robert." Did you know that? King is just plain King—unless you want to say it's a nickname for "Kingdom." But that's a stretch.

Second, remember our unit on World History when we learned about hieroglyphics? Cal wanted to find out how his name would look in pictures. Here's what the name generator showed him:

Circle + Arm + Lion = C A L !
Triple cool, ja?

next
page
↳

As for me, guess what the generator said about my name?

KALEY IS ALREADY A NICKNAME!!!

It's short for "Katherine," which just happens to be my middle name:
Kaley Katherine Bluster.

So, I've had a nickname ALL ALONG and I didn't even know it!
What a relief.

Merry Holidays to you and King Bob ☺

Just Plain Kaley (Forever)

KALEY's KORNER
(practicing for my "someday" Web site) :)

My hello list:

Hawaiian = aloha

Norwegian = goddag

French = bonjour

Croation = zdravo

Dutch = goedendag

Welsh = bore da

My list of "secret messages" to add to e-mail:

;)	wink	: *	kiss
#-)	not feeling well	:, (	crying
#:-o	shocked	:)	happy
%-(	confused	: (	sad
>:-(	mad	:-<	very sad
>:-<	really mad	:-C	very, very sad
>=^P	yuck!	:-#	wearing braces
<:-(	dunce	:-&	tongue-tied
(( ))+**	hugs and kisses	:-,	smirking
(::()::)	BAND-AID	:-@	screaming
*<:-)	Santa Claus	:-D	big smile
0:-)	angel	[:-I	Frankenstein
@>—-	a rose	:-r	sticking out tongue
~~8}	snake	~:o	baby
8-)	wearing glasses	:-x	my lips are sealed
8-O	wow!	I-O	yawning
: [	bored	:-}	mischievous smile
:( )	shouting	=O	surprised

"SLANGUAGE"

attt = and that's the truth
fwiw = for what it's worth
ttfn = ta-ta for now
cuwul = catch up with you later
ruok = are you okay?
bzzy = busy
yr = yeah, right
gtr = got to run
nm = never mind
tafn = that's all for now
h&k = hugs and kisses
adn = any day now
imo = in my opinion
gal = get a life
jk = just kidding
idk = I don't know
sh = same here
btw = by the way
thx = thanks
lol = laughing out loud
rolf = rolling on the floor, laughing
Clhtbtaaitmechg = Cal learned how to burp the alphabet and is
torturing me every chance he gets. (←okay, I made this one up)

E-mail
Rocks!

imo

KALEY's KALENDAR ☺

NOTES
(or other important
stuff to remember)

Shanay is
a cyberpal
stealer!

I wonder
if Lobo is
cute-o ♥

SUNDAY	MONDAY	TUESDAY
	1 Time to get computer privileges back!!	**2**
7 Memorize states and capitals (All 50 this time.)	**8** Social Studies quiz!	**9**
14	**15**	**16** Work on Kaley's Korner (My very own Web site!!!)
21 Movie night	**22**	**23** Return books to library
☺ **28** Dinner at Gma Bluster's (4 Mattie's 1/3 year bday)	**29**	**30** Ask Shanay how to put a guestbook on my site.

Kastles
R
Kewll!

WEDNESDAY	THURSDAY	FRIDAY	SATURDAY
3 Mr. S's birthday (I think) (Ask Ms. B.)	4	5 hai~~rc~~ut	6 Dad promised a mall day!
10	11	12 hai~~rc~~ut	13 Cal's Karate X-a-bi-shun
17	18	19 hai~~rc~~ut	20 haircut FINALLY! (Mom is toooo busy)
24	25 Mattie's 4 month birthday	26 Dentist ☹ Hope Mom Forgets Hope Mom Forgets Hope Mom Forgets	27
31	~~32~~ Oooops!		

My Good-bye List:

Arabic = salaam

French = au revoir

Tibetan = kali pai

Turkish = elveda

Zulu = sala kahle

Yiddish = zay gesunt

Swedish = adjö

Bon Voyage!!

brb

CYAL8ER